Skullabnes Island

Five Minutes to Bed!

Richard Dungworth ★ Sharon Harmer

The **pirate ship** bobbed gently
as the sun set in the sky,
When all who served aboard her
heard a timber-shivering cry...

"BEDTIME,
me hearties!"

"But Captain, **we're not tired yet**,

we're terrors of the seven seas!

We're rough tough noisy pirates,

just **five** more minutes, please!"

"Not tired?" Captain Cutlass said,
"Then very well, my crew,
Five minutes more can hardly hurt,
besides, there's lots to do!

There's a mast to mend
and rigging to check
and one of you terrors
can swab the deck!"

The **pirate ship** bobbed gently
as the twilight slowly fell,
When all who served aboard her
heard a gangplank-rattling yell...

"BEDTIME,
me hearties!"

"But Captain, **we're not tired yet**,

we're terrors of the seven seas!

We're rough tough noisy pirates,

just **four** more minutes, please!"

"**All right, all right,**" the captain cried,
"Pipe down, for pity's sake!
I'll let you have **four** minutes more,
but since you're wide awake…

There's a cannon to fix
and sails to patch
and timber to varnish
and rats to catch!"

The **pirate ship** bobbed gently
as the night began to fall,
When all who served aboard her
heard a jib-boom-jiggling bawl…

"BEDTIME,
me hearties!"

"But Captain, **we're not tired yet**,

we're terrors of the seven seas!

We're rough tough noisy pirates,

just **three** more minutes, please!"

"By barnacles!" the captain cried,
"**Three** minutes more, you ask?

Well, as things aren't quite shipshape,

I'll find you each a task…

There's treasure to count
and rope to coil
and portholes to polish
and chains to oil!"

The **pirate ship** bobbed gently
as the twinkling stars came out,
When all who served aboard her
heard a poopdeck-shuddering shout...

"BEDTIME,
me hearties!"

"But Captain, **we're not tired yet**,

we're terrors of the seven seas!

We're rough tough noisy pirates,

just **two** more minutes, please!"

"Enough, enough!" the captain cried,
"No need to go beserk.
Two minutes more will do no harm,
and so get back to work!"

There's washing to scrub
and hats to stitch
and cracks in the hull
to seal with pitch!"

The **pirate ship** bobbed gently
as the moon peeped round the sail,
When all who served aboard her
heard a cutlass-quivering wail…

"BeDTIME,
me hearties!"

But Captain, **we're not tired yet**,

we're terrors of the seven seas!

We're rough tough noisy pirates,

just **one** more minute, please!"

"**Suffering skiffs!**" the captain cried,

"All right – **one** minute more.

But since you're feeling full of beans,

I've chores for you galore!

There's supper to serve
and stores to stow
and cabins to tidy
down below!"

The **pirate ship** bobbed gently

in the moon's pale silver light,

While all who served aboard her

were as silent as the night…

"Not tired, shipmates? **Now** you are!

Sleep well, my rough tough crew.

And now, my little pirate…

...it's bedtime, too, for **YOU**!"

Raggedy Rocks

The Roaring Reef

Wicked Whirlpool

Mud Swamps

Spidery Jungle

Treasure Bay

Timber Bay

Parrot Park

Driftwood Dock

Skullabones Town

SKULLABONES ISLAND